Don't Wake Up Mama!

Another Five Little Monkeys Story

Eileen Christelow

A TRUMPET CLUB SPECIAL EDITION

For Bob, Karen, and Liza

Published by The Trumpet Club, Inc.,
a subsidiary of Bantam Doubleday Dell Publishing Group, Inc.,
1540 Broadway, New York, New York 10036.
"A Trumpet Club Special Edition" with the portrayal of a
trumpet and two circles is a registered trademark of
Bantam Doubleday Dell Publishing Group, Inc.

Text and illustrations copyright © 1992 by Eileen Christelow

ISBN 0-440-83371-X

This edition reprinted by special arrangement with Clarion Books,
a Houghton Mifflin Company imprint.

Printed in the United States of America
September 1994
5 7 9 10 8 6 4
UPR

Five little monkeys wake up with the sun.
"Today is Mama's birthday!"

3

Five little monkeys tiptoe past Mama sleeping.
"Let's bake a birthday cake!"

"Sh-h-h! Don't wake up Mama!"

One little monkey reads the recipe.

"Two cups of flour. Three teaspoons of baking powder.

"Sift everything together.
But don't sneeze! You'll wake up Mama!"

"Sh-h-h! Don't wake up Mama!"

Five little monkeys check on Mama.
"She's still asleep. We can finish making the cake."

One little monkey reads the recipe.
"Add four eggs."
Four little monkeys each get some eggs.

"And we need sugar and oil."
"Don't spill the oil!"

But one little monkey spills…

...And another little monkey slips and falls.
"Sh-h-h! Don't wake up Mama!"

Five little monkeys check on Mama.

"She's still asleep.

We can finish making the cake."

15

One little monkey reads the recipe.

"Next, mix everything together and put it into pans.

Then bake the cake in the oven."

Another little monkey says, "Now we can go up
to our room and make a present for Mama."

Five little monkeys start to make a present.

"Sh-h-h! Don't wake up Mama!"

One little monkey says, "Do you smell something burning?"

Five little monkeys race past Mama sleeping.
"Sh-h-h! Don't wake up Mama!"

"Oh no! The cake dripped all over."

"Turn off the oven!"

"Save the cake!"

"Sh-h-h! Don't wake up Mama!"

"Look! Here comes the fire engine!"
says one little monkey.
"Sh-h-h! Don't wake up Mama!"
says another little monkey.

"Where's the fire?"
shouts a fireman.
"It's not a fire!"
sniffs one little monkey.
"We ruined Mama's
birthday cake."

"Wait!" says another little monkey.
"This cake doesn't taste TOO bad."
"Frosting might help," says the
other fireman.

Five little monkeys and two firemen frost the cake.

"Now we can wake up Mama!"

Five little monkeys and two firemen
sing to Mama very, VERY, VERY LOUDLY.

And Mama wakes up!

"What a wonderful surprise," she says. "But my birthday is tomorrow!"

"Oh no!" say five little monkeys. "But can we still have birthday cake for breakfast?"

"Why not?" says Mama.

Five little monkeys, two firemen, and Mama think the birthday cake is delicious.

One little monkey whispers, "We can bake another cake tomorrow."

Another little monkey says, "Sh-h-h! Don't tell Mama!"